Who's Afraid of the Dark?

"Jessica's afraid of the dark," Charlie teased loudly. "Poor little Jessica."

Elizabeth's heart skipped a beat. She looked across the room. Everyone was staring at Jessica, whose face was turning pink.

"Isn't that pretty babyish?" Ken asked.

"You leave her alone, Ken," Elizabeth said. "You'd be scared too, if you had nightmares about monsters."

"Liz!" Jessica wailed.

"Monsters!" Winston yelled. He did a Frankenstein walk across the room, his legs stiff and his arms straight out. "Aaargh!" he growled.

"Quit it!" Jessica said angrily. Then she turned to her sister with tears in her eyes. "Why did you have to tell?"

Bantam Skylark Books in the SWEET VALLEY KIDS series

#1 SURPRISE! SURPRISE!
#2 RUNAWAY HAMSTER
#3 THE TWINS' MYSTERY TEACHER
#4 ELIZABETH'S VALENTINE
#5 JESSICA'S CAT TRICK
#6 LILA'S SECRET
#7 JESSICA'S BIG MISTAKE
#8 JESSICA'S ZOO ADVENTURE
#9 ELIZABETH'S SUPER-SELLING LEMONADE
#10 THE TWINS AND THE WILD WEST
#11 CRYBABY LOIS
#12 SWEET VALLEY TRICK OR TREAT
#13 STARRING WINSTON EGBERT
#14 JESSICA THE BABY-SITTER
#15 FEARLESS ELIZABETH
#16 JESSICA THE TV STAR
#17 CAROLINE'S MYSTERY DOLLS
#18 BOSSY STEVEN
#19 JESSICA AND THE JUMBO FISH
#20 THE TWINS GO TO THE HOSPITAL
#21 JESSICA AND THE SPELLING-BEE SURPRISE
#22 SWEET VALLEY SLUMBER PARTY
#23 LILA'S HAUNTED HOUSE PARTY
#24 COUSIN KELLY'S FAMILY SECRET
#25 LEFT-OUT ELIZABETH
#26 JESSICA'S SNOBBY CLUB
#27 THE SWEET VALLEY CLEANUP TEAM
#28 ELIZABETH MEETS HER HERO
#29 ANDY AND THE ALIEN
#30 JESSICA'S UNBURIED TREASURE
#31 ELIZABETH AND JESSICA RUN AWAY
#32 LEFT BACK!
#33 CAROLINE'S HALLOWEEN SPELL
#34 THE BEST THANKSGIVING EVER
#35 ELIZABETH'S BROKEN ARM
#36 ELIZABETH'S VIDEO FEVER
#37 THE BIG RACE
#38 GOOD-BYE, EVA?
#39 ELLEN IS HOME ALONE
#40 ROBIN IN THE MIDDLE
#41 THE MISSING TEA SET
#42 JESSICA'S MONSTER NIGHTMARE

SWEET VALLEY KIDS SUPER SNOOPER EDITIONS
#1 THE CASE OF THE SECRET SANTA
#2 THE CASE OF THE MAGIC CHRISTMAS BELL
#3 THE CASE OF THE HAUNTED CAMP
#4 THE CASE OF THE CHRISTMAS THIEF
#5 THE CASE OF THE HIDDEN TREASURE

SWEET VALLEY KIDS

JESSICA'S MONSTER NIGHTMARE

Written by
Molly Mia Stewart

Created by
FRANCINE PASCAL

Illustrated by
Ying-Hwa Hu

A BANTAM SKYLARK BOOK®
NEW YORK·TORONTO·LONDON·SYDNEY·AUCKLAND

RL 2, 005-008

JESSICA'S MONSTER NIGHTMARE
A Bantam Skylark Book / September 1993

Sweet Valley High® and Sweet Valley Kids are
trademarks of Francine Pascal

Conceived by Francine Pascal

Produced by Daniel Weiss Associates, Inc.
33 West 17th Street
New York, NY 10011

Cover art by Susan Tang

Skylark Books is a registered trademark of Bantam Books, a
division of Bantam Doubleday Dell Publishing Group, Inc.
Registered in U.S. Patent and Trademark Office and elsewhere.

ISBN: 0-553-48008-1

Published simultaneously in the United States and Canada

Bantam Books are published by Bantam Books, a division of Bantam
Doubleday Dell Publishing Group, Inc. Its trademark, consisting of the
words "Bantam Books" and the portrayal of a rooster, is Registered in
U.S. Patent and Trademark Office and in other countries. Marca
Registrada. Bantam Books, 1540 Broadway, New York, New York 10036.

PRINTED IN THE UNITED STATES OF AMERICA

CWO   0 9 8 7 6 5 4 3 2 1

CHAPTER 1

Keep the Light On

Elizabeth Wakefield pulled the bed-spread up to her chin and pretended to shiver.

"The end," Mr. Wakefield said, closing the cover of the Grimms' fairy-tale book.

"I didn't like that one. It was creepy," said Jessica, Elizabeth's twin sister. She hugged her koala bear tight.

Mr. Wakefield kissed her forehead. "We can read a happy one tomorrow, honey. Now, go to sleep, you two."

Elizabeth snuggled in bed with her own koala bear as her father tucked her in. Elizabeth's and Jessica's koalas were identical, just as Elizabeth and Jessica were. Being twins meant that the girls looked exactly alike. Both had blue-green eyes and long blond hair with bangs. When they wore matching outfits to school, even their best friends had trouble telling them apart. Only by checking the name bracelets each twin wore could anyone be sure who was who.

But below the surface, each girl was different and special in her own way. Elizabeth loved sports and making up adventure games to play in the backyard. She was a good student and worked hard in all of her classes. Jessica was smart too, but she thought school was boring. She passed notes to her friends and liked to pretend she was a movie star during recess.

Despite their differences, though, Elizabeth and Jessica were best friends. They always looked out for each other, and knew when the other was unhappy or worried.

"Good night, Dad," Elizabeth said.

Mr. Wakefield turned off the light and closed the door behind him. Instantly Jessica was out of bed. She ran across the room and switched the light back on.

"What are you doing?" Elizabeth

asked. "It's time to go to sleep."

Jessica climbed back into bed. "Oh, umm . . . I want to read for a few minutes."

"Read?" Elizabeth repeated in surprise.

Jessica looked around, then picked up Elizabeth's *Hedgehog Lodge* book from the night table. Elizabeth's eyebrows went up. "You never read my books. What's happening to you?"

"Sure I do," Jessica said. "Anyway, you're always saying how good this book is." She opened to the first page, then quickly turned to page two. It seemed as though she was only pretending to read.

"How long are you going to stay up?" Elizabeth asked.

Jessica looked at her sister with wide eyes. "Not very long. I just want to finish this chapter."

"Then can I turn off the light?" Elizabeth asked.

"NO!" Jessica threw the book down on her bed and ran across the room to stand in front of the light switch. "Don't turn off the light!" she begged.

Elizabeth sat up straight in bed. "What's wrong?"

Jessica shook her head. "Nothing."

"I *know* something's wrong," Elizabeth said. "What is it?"

Jessica sniffled. "The story Dad read made me . . . scared," she said. "It reminded me of that ugly monster we saw in the picture book at Mrs. Taylor's

house." Mrs. Taylor was an old family friend whose house they had visited recently.

Elizabeth nodded. "But it was just a picture," she pointed out.

"I know." Jessica twisted a strand of her hair. "But then I saw part of that scary movie Steven was watching yesterday, and last night I had a *horrible* nightmare. I don't want to go to sleep again."

"But you have to sleep. Nobody can stay awake forever," Elizabeth said.

"I can," Jessica said stubbornly.

Elizabeth could tell Jessica was very serious. "Jess, you know there's no such thing as monsters, right? And a dream can't hurt you."

"I know, but . . ." Jessica looked over her shoulder.

"You can wake me up if you start to have a bad dream," Elizabeth promised. "OK?"

"Well . . . OK," Jessica said uncertainly.

"So can I turn off the light?" Elizabeth got out of bed and stood by her sister.

Jessica hesitated. "I guess it's all right," she said finally.

Elizabeth smiled. "Get in bed. I'll turn off the light when you're ready."

Slowly Jessica got into bed and pulled the covers up high. She stared at the ceiling. "I'm ready."

Elizabeth turned off the light.

CHAPTER 2

Nightmare!

Jessica lay staring at the ceiling. Her eyes were wide open. She knew it was babyish for a seven-year-old to be afraid of the dark, but she was one-hundred-percent positive that if she fell asleep, she would have the same terrible nightmare she had had the night before.

I just won't fall asleep, she thought nervously.

She could hear her heartbeat thumping in her ears. A car went by outside, and its headlights swept across the ceiling from the window. Jessica turned her head.

"Liz?" she whispered.

There was no answer. Jessica pulled the covers up even higher. Maybe if she tried to think of nice things, she would stay awake, she decided.

Jessica listed all her favorite colors from her crayon box. "Carnation, magenta, aquamarine," she whispered softly, "apricot, sky . . ." Her eyes closed.

Then Jessica jerked awake again, her heart pounding. She had almost fallen asleep!

For a moment she thought about waking up Elizabeth. But Elizabeth wasn't afraid of anything, and Jessica knew she should try to be just as brave. She decided to think about happy things.

Kittens, puppies, ducklings, bunnies . . .

Jessica closed her eyes and hugged her koala bear. *Lambs, baby otters, lion cubs . . .*

She drifted off, chasing three adorable lion cubs around a playground. One of them crawled through a hole in a wall, and Jessica knew she had to get it. She crawled in on her hands and knees and found herself in a dark, spooky tunnel. The lion cub was nowhere to be seen. Quickly she turned around and around, looking for a way out.

Then she heard a low growl. A shiver went up her spine. Jessica was certain it wasn't the lion cub. It was a monster. Again she looked for a way to get out. The ground was beginning to shake, and the monster's growl sounded nastier than ever. Jessica began to run, holding out her hands in case she hit something in the dark. But no matter how hard she ran, she never seemed to get anywhere. The monster was chasing her, getting closer with every second.

"Oh, no!" Jessica wailed, feeling her feet get heavier with each step she took. She looked back over her shoulder, and then—there it was!

The monster filled up the whole tunnel behind her. It was so big that its giant head touched the ceiling. Each one of its three eyes looked in a different direction, trying to find her. Jessica was so terror-stricken that she couldn't move. In a moment it would see her.

Jessica screamed and waved her arms wildly—and sat straight up in bed.

"What is it, Jess?" Elizabeth asked, waking up. "Are you all right?"

"Liz! It was the monster!" Jessica cried, climbing out of her bed and getting into Elizabeth's. "It was awful!"

Elizabeth held Jessica's sweaty hand. "Do you want to tell me about it?"

"No!" Jessica whispered. She could still feel her heart racing. But she wanted Elizabeth to know she wasn't just being a baby. "It really was horrible."

"What happened?"

"I was in a dark, spooky tunnel," Jessica explained, squeezing her sister's hand tight. "I knew the monster was behind me, and then I saw it."

"Go on," Elizabeth whispered.

Jessica swallowed. "It was chasing me," she continued in a frightened voice. "Just like last night. So far I've gotten away, but I know something horrible will happen if I don't. I'm afraid the next time the monster will catch me and eat me up."

"Then it'll have to eat me, too," Elizabeth said bravely. "I'll go with you next time, and maybe if we're together we can escape from it."

"Really?" Jessica was beginning to feel much better, knowing that she was

14

with her twin sister. She yawned. "Promise?"

"Promise."

In the dark, they each crossed their hearts and snapped their fingers twice. It was their special promise sign. Jessica reached for Elizabeth's hand again, and a little while later, she fell asleep.

CHAPTER 3

Jessica's Afraid of the Dark

Elizabeth walked into Mrs. Otis's class before the bell the next morning. She looked back over her shoulder.

"Come on, Jess," she said.

Jessica followed slowly behind her. Then, in the doorway, Jessica stopped and yawned wide enough for Elizabeth to see down Jessica's throat.

"What's wrong with Jessica?" Amy Sutton asked as Elizabeth got to her desk.

Elizabeth put her books down and glanced back at her sister. Jessica was standing with Lila Fowler and Ellen Riteman, two of her best friends. But she wasn't talking.

"She didn't sleep well last night," Elizabeth said. "I feel bad for her."

"Why?" Amy looked puzzled.

Eva Simpson joined them, and Elizabeth decided to ask them both for advice. "Jessica can't sleep anymore," she explained. "All of a sudden she's afraid of the dark."

"That's too bad," Eva said. "Did something scare her?"

Elizabeth glanced around again to make sure nobody was listening. She didn't want to embarrass her sister.

17

She leaned closer to her friends.

"She's been having nightmares. About a monster."

"Jessica's having monster nightmares?" Amy repeated.

Sandy Ferris, who was walking by, stopped. "Jessica has nightmares about monsters?" she asked in disbelief.

"What?" Caroline Pearce overheard Sandy and came over. She was always trying to listen in on everyone's private conversations.

"I don't want a whole lot of people to know," Elizabeth said anxiously.

"Yeah," Sandy agreed. "I bet Jessica wouldn't want anyone to know she's afraid of the dark."

Three boys sitting near the window

18

suddenly looked over. Charlie Cashman began to grin. "Jessica's afraid of the dark," he teased loudly. "Poor little Jessica."

Elizabeth's heart skipped a beat. She looked across the room. Everyone was staring at Jessica, whose face was turning pink.

"Isn't that pretty babyish?" Ken Matthews asked Jessica.

"You leave her alone, Ken," Elizabeth said. "You'd be scared too, if you had nightmares about monsters."

"Liz!" Jessica wailed.

"Monsters!" Winston Egbert yelled. "Watch this." He did a Frankenstein walk across the room, his legs stiff and his arms straight out. "Aaarghh!" he growled.

"Quit it!" Jessica said angrily.

But it was too late. All the boys began making monster faces and sound effects, and pretended to attack Jessica. Elizabeth felt terrible. She went to stand next to Jessica.

"Cut it out," she warned as her friend Todd Wilkins shuffled over in a hunchback position.

"You're not afraid of *monsters*, are you?" Todd whispered in a deep voice. He laughed and ran back to his desk.

Jessica had tears in her eyes. "Why did you have to tell?" she asked Elizabeth.

"It was an accident, honest," Elizabeth apologized. "I wish I'd never opened my mouth."

21

The monster sound effects continued, and Jessica looked as though she was about to burst into tears. Then Mrs. Otis came in. Instantly, the boys stood still, looking innocent.

"Take your seats, class," Mrs. Otis said, looking around suspiciously.

Elizabeth and Jessica walked to their desks. After attendance, their teacher made an announcement.

"As you know, Parent-Teacher Night is coming up soon," Mrs. Otis said. "The school is going to have a poster contest, with one poster from each classroom to be chosen for the entrance display. We'll spend some time tomorrow in art class working on our designs."

"That'll be fun, won't it?" Elizabeth

whispered to Jessica with a hopeful smile.

Jessica shrugged. She yawned again. "I don't care."

Elizabeth wished there was a way to cheer up her sister. She glanced at Mrs. Otis. Normally, Elizabeth would never pass a note in class, but this was an emergency.

She pulled a piece of paper from her notebook and drew a happy face on it. Then underneath it she wrote, "Jessica Wakefield." She folded it up and quickly put it on her sister's desk.

Jessica slowly unfolded the note. She stared at it for a moment. Then she picked up her pencil and drew a dark frown over the smile.

CHAPTER 4

A Big Scare

After dinner Jessica curled up on the couch to watch a game show. Elizabeth was working on poster designs.

"What's on TV?" the twins' older brother, Steven, asked as he came in. He picked up the remote control and switched the channel to a science-fiction show.

Jessica frowned. "Hey, who said you could do that?"

"I did," Steven said. He put the remote control in his sweatshirt pocket.

Jessica looked at the television. A group of space explorers were in a cave, tiptoeing toward a light. "I don't want to watch this," she said.

"It's better than the game show," Steven insisted.

"But I wanted to watch—" Jessica broke off in midsentence and stared at the television. A low grumbling was coming from the dark cave. She felt her heart speed up.

"This is cool," Steven said. "There's an awesome alien that comes out and eats one of the space explorers."

Elizabeth quickly looked up from her sketchbook to watch the screen. Then she looked at Jessica.

"Steven, I think we should switch the channel," Elizabeth said in a loud voice.

"Why?" Steven asked. "Just because you say so?"

"No, because this is scaring Jess," Elizabeth answered. "She's been having a bad monster dream, and this will make her have another one."

Jessica frowned. "Quit telling everybody!" she snapped.

"But he should know why he's being mean," Elizabeth said.

"Jessica's having monster dreams?" Steven asked with a grin. "Poor Jessie-Wessie, scared of the big bad monsters." He crossed his eyes and stuck out his tongue.

"What's going on?" Mrs. Wakefield

asked as she hurried into the den.

"Steven's trying to scare me," Jessica said. All of a sudden she burst into tears. Mrs. Wakefield sat down and hugged her.

"What's wrong, Jess?" she asked gently.

Sniffing, Jessica rubbed her cheek against her mother's shoulder. "I—I had a bad dream over and over—about a monster," she sobbed.

"I told her there's no such thing, but it didn't help," Elizabeth said.

As Jessica was telling her mother how awful the monster was, Mr. Wakefield came in too. Jessica began crying all over again when he asked what was wrong.

"She's afraid of the dark," Steven said. "She's afraid a vampire is going to get her."

"Not a vampire!" Jessica said. "A big monster."

"Puck, puck, puck, puck, puck." Steven flapped his arms as he imitated a chicken.

"That's enough, Steven," their father said sternly.

"Now, honey," Mrs. Wakefield said, giving Jessica a protective hug. "You know that we're all here, and that you're safe, don't you?"

Jessica sniffled a little bit and nodded.

"Although we sometimes have bad dreams, they can't hurt us. They're just in our imagination," Mrs. Wakefield continued.

"I know," Jessica said. She was beginning to feel sleepy, and much less afraid. "I'm a big girl," she added.

"That's right, you are," her mother said. "Now, how about getting into bed? Do you think you're ready?"

Jessica looked at Elizabeth. "Well . . ."

"Come on," Elizabeth said. "It'll be easy."

"OK," Jessica agreed at last.

"That's a good brave girl," Mr. Wakefield said.

Jessica went up the stairs one at a time. Very slowly she put on her pajamas, and very, very slowly she brushed her teeth. Elizabeth was already in bed. Then Mrs. Wakefield told them a happy bedtime story to cheer Jessica up.

"I'm going to turn off the light now," Mrs. Wakefield said when she was finished. "Ready?"

Jessica gulped hard. She knew she would get teased as long as she was afraid of the dark. But she felt more confident. "Ready," she whispered.

"Good night, girls," Mrs. Wakefield said, and then she turned off the light.

"I'm not afraid," Jessica said in the darkness.

"I know," Elizabeth whispered.

Jessica snuggled down. She was already very sleepy, and she was sure she would have no trouble dozing off. All she had to do was think of nice things, like rainbows and unicorns, and . . .

"RRRAAUGH!" came a ferocious bellow.

Jessica sat straight up in bed and screamed. A horrible monster was standing in the doorway of the room!

"Steven!" Elizabeth yelled.

Steven pulled a rubber ghoul mask off his face and laughed. "You were so scared, Jess! Baby!"

Jessica tried hard not to cry, but Steven had frightened her badly.

"What's going on in there?" Mr. Wakefield demanded as he came up the stairs and rushed into the room.

"Steven came in and scared me!" Jessica wailed.

Steven was beginning to look a little bit scared himself. "It was just a joke," he said nervously.

Mr. Wakefield pointed to the door. "Go to your room, Steven. I'll be in to talk to you in a minute."

"Yes, sir," Steven said.

Jessica lay back down. "I'm not afraid," she whispered. "I'm not afraid."

"Do you want to sleep with your night-table light on?" Mr. Wakefield asked kindly.

"No, I'm not afraid," Jessica repeated in a quavery voice.

"You're sure?" Elizabeth asked.

Jessica squeezed her eyes shut and nodded. She knew the monster would come. But she didn't want to be scared.

CHAPTER 5

Poster Time

Elizabeth woke up in the dark. At first she didn't know what had woken her. Then she heard it again—a soft, muffled sob.

"Jessica?" she whispered.

"I dreamed about the m-monster," Jessica said tearfully.

"I know," Elizabeth said. "I can tell." That special understanding that twins shared was working. Elizabeth felt frightened too.

"What am I going to do?" Jessica wondered.

Jessica sounded so sad and so worried that Elizabeth stopped being frightened and just felt angry. "I hate that monster," she said. "I'll help you, I promise."

"Really?" Jessica asked.

"Really." Elizabeth reached into the dark space between their beds. "Here's my hand."

Jessica took her hand and held tight. "I'll tell you a story," Elizabeth said. "Once upon a time—"

"There aren't any monsters in it, are there?" Jessica broke in hastily.

Elizabeth shook her head on her pillow. "Not even a teeny, tiny, itsy-bitsy monster with a stuffy nose."

Jessica giggled. "OK. Tell the story."

Quietly, in the dark, Elizabeth made up a story for Jessica. And bit by bit, Jessica's fingers loosened around Elizabeth's. At last they both fell fast asleep again.

The next day in school, Mrs. Otis taped large pieces of poster board on the walls of the classroom. "Everyone choose a position and draw," she said. "I have to step out for about twenty minutes. Mr. Frankel from next door will look in on you. Happy drawing."

Elizabeth took her favorite marker from her desk. "I already know what I'm going to draw," she said to Amy. "A picture of the ocean, with whales and dolphins."

"I'm drawing an elephant parade," Amy said.

Elizabeth looked around. Some of the kids were drawing animals. Caroline Pearce was drawing a bunch of balloons. Then she saw that Todd was drawing a purple Frankenstein head.

"Hey," Elizabeth said, walking over to him. "Do you have to draw that?"

"Why shouldn't I? I'm really good at drawing monsters," he replied. "All that kidding around yesterday gave me the idea."

Elizabeth looked around the room and saw that several other boys were drawing space aliens and monsters too. She just hoped they wouldn't begin to tease Jessica again.

"Don't you have any ideas yet?" she asked, walking back to her spot next to her sister.

Jessica was staring gloomily at her blank poster board. "No," she said, sighing. "All I can think of is the monster."

"Hey, I used to dream about a monster too," Winston said. "That was when I was a little kid, though."

Jessica looked down at her sneakers. Elizabeth liked Winston, but right now she wished he would go away.

"Do you want to see what it looked like?" Winston asked, taking a piece of paper from a pile of art supplies on a desk. "Here, I'll show you."

He bent over the desk to draw his own scary nightmare monster. Elizabeth watched over his shoulder. Winston's picture looked more like a big fat frog than a scary creature.

"You were afraid of that?" Ken asked, taking a look. "If I dreamed of that, I'd laugh."

"It was when I was a kid," Winston explained.

"Hey, Jessica," Charlie asked. "If your monster looks like Win's, you're a bigger baby than I thought."

"Cut it out, Charlie," Elizabeth said fiercely.

Jessica was still staring at the floor, not speaking.

"Why don't you draw your monster?" Ken taunted. "Go on. We want to see how funny-looking it is."

"It isn't funny-looking," Jessica said in a low voice.

"Leave her alone," Elizabeth insisted.

"Come on, Jessica," Todd joined in. "Why don't you show us? Or are you too afraid to do even that?"

Before Elizabeth had time to stand up for her sister, there was a crowd all around them. Everyone wanted Jessica to draw her scary monster. And deep down, Elizabeth was curious to know what it looked like too.

Finally Jessica looked around at the group teasing her. "You don't believe that it's really a horrible, terrifying monster," she said. "But I'll show you."

CHAPTER 6

Truly Frightening

Jessica looked at the blank poster board. Then she took a deep breath, picked out a marker, and squeezed her eyes shut. Half of her wanted to imagine the monster. The other half definitely did not.

But she wanted to prove she really had something to fear. She opened her eyes.

"Does it have a face?" Elizabeth asked.

"Yes." Jessica began to draw the outline of the monster.

"What color is it?" Sandy asked.

"Is it hairy or slimy or like a lizard?" Andy Franklin asked.

Jessica frowned hard in concentration. It was good to know that she was surrounded by all her friends while she drew her monster. The common-sense part of her knew it couldn't get her. But there was another part of her that was scared anyway.

"This is what it's like," she said quietly while she filled in some details.

"It's disgusting," Lila said with a shiver.

When Jessica was done, she stepped back to examine her picture from a distance. She didn't like what she saw. It was exactly like the monster of her nightmare.

Its shape was a similar to a bear's, and it took up almost the whole poster board. Three eyes stared out from its huge head, and it had long, jagged fangs for teeth. Its hands were raised up as though to catch someone with its sharp claws. The body was covered with scales, and it had a thin, ratlike, pointed tail.

"Those eyes are creepy," Winston said, stepping to one side. "No matter where you are, they look at you."

Nobody else said anything for a moment. They were all looking at Jessica's drawing.

Then Amy spoke up. "If I dreamed

that was chasing me, I'd be scared too."

"See?" Jessica said. She was glad she had proved how horrible the monster was.

But there was still one gigantic problem. She was still afraid of the dark.

CHAPTER 7

A Monster to Laugh At

During reading period, the class was quiet, with all the students bent over their books. Elizabeth looked at the monster poster. Then she looked at Jessica. Jessica had her head down on the desk, on top of her open book.

"Jess?" Elizabeth whispered.

Jessica didn't answer. Mrs. Otis stood up and walked between the desks.

"Jessica?" the teacher said quietly, touching Jessica's shoulder.

"Hmm?" Jessica raised her head and blinked. "What?"

"Come with me, Jessica," Mrs. Otis said. She took Jessica's hand and led her to the front of the room. Worried, Elizabeth watched, and wondered what was wrong.

By Mrs. Otis's desk, Jessica and the teacher had a whispered conversation. Jessica nodded and rubbed her eyes sleepily. Then Mrs. Otis wrote something on a piece of paper. Jessica took it and left the room.

Elizabeth couldn't stand the suspense any longer. She hurried up to the teacher.

"Is Jessica in trouble?" she asked nervously.

"No," Mrs. Otis replied. "I sent her to the nurse's office to take a nap. I've never seen her so tired."

Elizabeth nodded. She felt sorry for Jessica, but she didn't know what to say.

"Is anything wrong at home?" Mrs. Otis asked in her kind, gentle voice.

"Jessica can't sleep at night," Elizabeth explained. She pointed to the poster. "She keeps having nightmares about that monster, so she's afraid of the dark and afraid to go to sleep."

Mrs. Otis looked at the picture for a long time without speaking. Then she shook her head and sighed. "I'm not surprised. It's a very frightening monster."

"I hate it," Elizabeth burst out. "It's ruining everything."

Mrs. Otis nodded. "I wonder if there's anything we can do," she said.

"I tried," Elizabeth said. "But Jess keeps dreaming about it and waking up all scared."

"Then we have to make the monster less horrible," Mrs. Otis said. "I have an idea."

The teacher picked up a marker from her desk and walked over to Jessica's poster. She leaned over and began drawing circles coming from the monster's ears.

"What's that?" Elizabeth asked.

"Soap bubbles." Mrs. Otis chuckled.

Elizabeth stared at the picture. "Soap

bubbles?" she repeated. Then a wide, excited smile spread across her face. "I get it."

She picked out a red crayon from a box on the table, and carefully drew a floppy red bow around the monster's neck. She stood back and giggled.

"Now it doesn't look quite so scary," Mrs. Otis said.

"Can I draw something on it too?" Andy asked.

Elizabeth and Mrs. Otis turned around in surprise. The whole class was watching them eagerly. Mrs. Otis looked at Elizabeth with a questioning smile.

"Everyone should add something," Elizabeth decided.

"Oh, I know what I'd put on!"

Caroline said, raising her hand.

One by one, and then two and three at a time, the kids in the class left their desks and crowded around Jessica's monster. First Andy drew round glasses for the three eyes. Then Lila added high-heeled blue and pink polka-dotted shoes. Next Eva put a large, swirly peppermint lollipop in one of the hands. Ken drew a baseball cap with a peace sign on the front. Everyone was beginning to laugh and call out suggestions. The best artists in class drew in the goofy details that the others were shouting. Elizabeth stood back, watching the monster turn from horrifying to hysterical. She couldn't help laughing.

"And the final touch," Mrs. Otis announced. She took a bottle of pink nail polish from her purse and painted it onto the monster's claws. Everyone howled with laughter.

"Nobody could be scared of that!" Amy said.

Elizabeth crossed her fingers behind her back. "I sure hope you're right."

CHAPTER 8

A Surprised Jessica

Jessica lay on the nurse's couch, staring at the ceiling. There was a checkerboard pattern up there, and she tried counting the squares. She even tried adding in her head, but she was too sleepy and too nervous to concentrate.

After drawing the monster for her class, it was more vivid in her imagination than before.

"Nurse?" she called out in a timid voice. She sat up and looked around at the first-aid diagrams and emergency phone numbers. She didn't want to take a nap, and she didn't want to stay there. It gave her goose bumps.

"Yes, Jessica? Are you feeling better now?" the nurse asked, coming in.

Jessica nodded quickly. "I feel fine," she said, trying not to yawn. "I'm ready to go back to class."

"If you're sure you feel better, go ahead," the school nurse replied with a friendly smile. "Be sure to get a good night's sleep this evening."

"I'll try," Jessica said. She ran out the door and hurried down the hallway to Mrs. Otis's classroom.

Just outside the door, she stopped. She knew that the moment she stepped inside, the monster poster would be staring back at her.

"I just won't look at it," she whispered. "I'll just pretend it isn't even there."

She opened the door and went in. Mrs. Otis turned from the blackboard in surprise. "Well, I didn't expect to see you back so soon."

Jessica shrugged. "I feel better," she said quietly. She turned to go back to her desk. It seemed as though everyone in class was looking at her and expecting her to say something. She glanced around.

"Notice anything?" Lila spoke up excitedly. Almost everyone was smiling, as if they all knew a secret.

Jessica looked at the blackboard. It

had the usual math problems on it. She looked at the desks. Everyone was sitting in their usual seats. She looked at the walls. All the posters were still there, including one that she didn't remember seeing before.

Then she gasped. "What happened? Is that my poster?"

Jessica could hardly believe her eyes. The monster that had started out so terrifying now looked like a crazy circus clown. It was almost impossible to recognize the horrible beast she had drawn.

"We fixed it up for you," Elizabeth explained. "We made it so the monster isn't scary anymore."

Jessica walked over to the poster for a closer look, and the other students stood around to point things out.

"I added that," Ellen said proudly, putting her finger on the heart-shaped barrettes in the monster's ponytails.

Mrs. Otis put her arm across Jessica's shoulder. "Now all you have to do when you're dreaming is remember that this is what the monster looks like now," she said. "And you'll laugh when you see it, instead of being scared."

Jessica nodded slowly, still looking at all the details. She noticed the fingernail polish and giggled. "Is it going to a party?" she asked.

"Yes," Elizabeth said cheerfully. "But when it gets there, it's the only one not wearing nice clothes."

"Wouldn't you die of embarrassment?"

Lila asked, laughing. "I would."

Jessica pointed to the soap bubbles. "That's what happens when it gets embarrassed," she said. "Bubbles come out of its ears."

Everyone laughed, and Jessica began to feel much better. "I bet if I dream about this monster, I won't be scared one little bit."

"Excellent!" Elizabeth said.

Todd gave Jessica a high-five, and Jessica gave Mrs. Otis a hug.

"You'll be fine, Jessica," their teacher said. "I'm certain."

"Me, too," Jessica said.

Then she met Elizabeth's eyes. They were both thinking the same thing.

The final test would be at bedtime.

CHAPTER 9

Tinkertops

After dinner, the whole Wakefield family watched television in the den. But instead of watching the comedy show, Elizabeth was actually watching Jessica.

Was it her imagination, or was her sister beginning to look a little bit nervous? Jessica glanced at the clock and fidgeted with the remote control. Their bedtime was in fifteen minutes.

"You're not getting afraid again, are

you?" Elizabeth whispered in Jessica's ear.

"N-no," Jessica said.

"Not even a little?" Elizabeth asked.

Jessica shrugged her shoulders. "Maybe a little bit," she admitted.

"Remember how the monster had those high-heeled shoes on?" Elizabeth said quickly. "Wasn't that funny?"

"Yes." Jessica nodded and smiled a very small smile. She glanced at the clock again.

"And remember the sign on its tail that said 'Kick Me?'" Elizabeth went on. "Think about all the goofy stuff like that."

"What's all this about?" Mr. Wakefield asked. "Last I heard, that monster was horrifying to look at. But from the sound of it, I'd say it looked pretty funny now."

"It does, Dad," Elizabeth said. "See, Jessica drew her monster in class, and we all added things so it wouldn't be scary anymore. And it isn't, right, Jess?"

"Right," Jessica agreed uncertainly.

"I think that's an excellent way to chase away monsters," their mother said. "Dress them up in silly clothes and make fun of them."

"Does it have a name?" Steven asked. He was being extra nice to make up for scaring Jessica.

Jessica shook her head. "No," she whispered. "It's just a monster."

"Come on," Steven said. "It has to

have a name. A really *stupid* name. Nobody can be scared of someone named—" He stopped for a moment to think. "Named Wilbur!"

Elizabeth nodded. "Or Myrtle. Or Flapjack Head."

"Or Slimenose!" Steven laughed and slapped his knee.

Jessica smiled. "Or Bubblebrain."

"Hey, Bubblebrain Slimenose!" Elizabeth said. "Get out of here, you dumb old *unscary* monster with nail polish."

Jessica let out a giggle. "Beat it, Slimacious Pinhead High-heels!" she shouted.

"Bad-breath Bowtie!" Elizabeth laughed.

Soon they were all laughing and shouting out the silliest names they

could think of, and Jessica was laughing the hardest of all.

"I know, I know—this is the real name," she announced, catching her breath and smiling from ear to ear. "Toodle-loo Tinkertops!"

Elizabeth fell off the arm of the couch and lay on the floor laughing. "I wish I could have the same dream. It would be so funny!"

"Well, how about it, then?" Mrs. Wakefield asked. "Who's ready for bed?"

Elizabeth stood up. She looked at her sister. "I am," she said.

"Me, too," Jessica said, getting to her feet. "I'll race you upstairs." She dashed out of the room.

"Hey!" Elizabeth started to follow,

and then looked back. "I think it worked," she said in a hopeful voice.

"Steven's idea was excellent," Mr. Wakefield agreed. "Giving that monster a name was the best way to take all the fear out of it."

Elizabeth let out her breath in a happy sigh. "Are you going to tuck us in?" she asked their parents.

"We'll be up in a moment," Mrs. Wakefield told her.

Elizabeth ran up the stairs to their bedroom. Jessica was already in bed, and she didn't look nervous at all.

"Thumbs-up?" Elizabeth said, giving Jessica the sign.

Jessica raised her thumb too. "Look out, Tinkertops, you sillyhead!"

Elizabeth quickly brushed her teeth and changed into her pajamas. Then Mr. and Mrs. Wakefield both came to tuck them in.

"Sweet dreams, girls," Mrs. Wakefield said, giving Jessica a kiss.

Mr. Wakefield reached for the light switch. "OK?" he asked.

"NO!"

Jessica jumped out of bed, and Elizabeth felt the smile vanish from her face. Jessica put her hand over the light switch.

"I want to turn it off myself," Jessica said with a grin.

CHAPTER 10

A Class Effort

Jessica sat upright in bed and blinked at the bright morning sunshine. "Liz!" she called urgently.

Elizabeth rolled over and opened her eyes. "What? What happened?"

"I didn't dream a single dream all night!" Jessica announced. "I even *wanted* to dream about Toodle-loo Tinkertops, but I didn't!"

Elizabeth smiled. "Does this mean you're not afraid of the dark anymore?"

"No way. That's just for babies," Jessica said confidently as she got out of bed. "I'm not afraid of anything!"

Jessica couldn't wait to tell her friends and Mrs. Otis that she wasn't frightened of her monster.

"And best of all, his name is Toodle-loo Tinkertops," she told Mrs. Otis proudly when she had finished the story for the teacher and the rest of the class.

Mrs. Otis smiled. "Well, I'm very glad to know he has a name," she said.

"Why, Mrs. Otis?" Elizabeth asked. She looked around the room. "Hey, the poster isn't here anymore!"

"I have a surprise," Mrs. Otis explained in a mysterious voice. "It's about Tinkertops."

Everyone in the class was silent. Jessica leaned forward with curiosity.

"The poster was picked to represent our class for Parent-Teacher Night," Mrs. Otis said. "It's about to be hung up in the front entrance."

"Really?" Jessica jumped up and down with excitement. "My own monster, out of my own imagination?"

"That's right," Mrs. Otis said. "But what makes it even better is that it was a true class effort."

"Everyone added something to the poster," Elizabeth said.

"That's excellent," Jessica said happily. "I wonder what I'll dream of next!"

*　　*　　*

"Maybe I'll be the monster from our class poster," Eva Simpson said when they were playing at the park that afternoon. Halloween was coming up, and costumes were being discussed.

"I'm more excited about going to the amusement park," Elizabeth said. "I love class trips. And everyone says the haunted house is really haunted."

"I don't believe it," Jessica said. She was proud not be afraid anymore. "I bet nothing happens to anyone."

"Girls," Charlie Cashman said as he rode by on his bicycle and pulled Jessica's hair. He was one of the biggest boys in their class and often bullied people. "You're wimps."

Jessica stood with her hands on her hips. "Get lost, Charlie," she yelled as he circled back and stopped in front of them. "You may be big, but you don't scare me."

Will Jessica stand up to Charlie's bullying ways at the amusement park? Find out in Sweet Valley Kids #43, **JESSICA GETS SPOOKED.**